For Anne Sylvestre, absolutely, and for Xavier's "you'll see, you'll see, everything will turn out all right." And for L. I. of "l'espace." —Thomas Scotto

www.enchantedlion.com

First English-language edition published in 2018 by Enchanted Lion Books
67 West Street, 317A, Brooklyn, NY 11222
Copyright © 2018 for the English-language translation by Enchanted Lion Books
Text and illustrations copyright © 2009 by Actes Sud
First published in French as "Jérôme par coeur"
All rights reserved under International and Pan-American Copyright Conventions.
A CIP record is on file with the Library of Congress. ISBN 978-1-59270-250-3

Printed in China by RR Donnelley Asia Printing Solutions Ltd.

1 3 5 7 9 10 8 6 4 2

Jerome By Heart

"And the passers-by pointed
their fingers at them.
But the children who love each other
aren't there for anyone else."
—Jacques Prévert

Words by Thomas Scotto

Illustrations by Olivier Tallec

Translated from the French by Claudia Zoe Bedrick & Karin Snelson

ENCHANTED LION BOOKS
NEW YORK

He always holds my hand.
It's true.
Really tight.

On field trips to the art museum,
it's me he chooses as his buddy.

That's why I love Jerome.

It doesn't bother me at all.
Raphael loves Jerome.
I can say it.
It's easy.

My mom thinks Jerome is very polite.

"So, so charming."

But she never says anything about how warm his smile is.

She doesn't seem to notice that I have a secret hideout there,

where I feel protected by Jerome's two eyes.

My dad thinks it's "a pity"
that Jerome doesn't play soccer.
But just because Jerome doesn't play rough
doesn't mean he's not strong.
He is strong.

"Hi, Raphael!"
Jerome always sees me,
even when he's with his friends.

"Want some?"
He always shares his snacks with me.

"Hey! Stop that!"
He defends me when kids make fun of me.
Incredible, right?

He also makes up stories that are so good
they seem real, so...

I've made up my mind.
From now on, every day is for Jerome.

Mornings are happy from the start!
By lunch, we've laughed so hard our stomachs hurt.
And by dinner, I've stocked up on enough of Jerome to last me the whole night.
That's important.

This morning at breakfast, I burst out:

"I had the best dream last night!

It was good in a Jerome kind of way."

Dad stares at his shoelaces, like he doesn't hear a word I'm saying.

Mom digs through my backpack and sighs,

"Eat your cereal, Raphael."

"Maybe I'll just eat my dream on toast!"

I'm joking, of course.

"That way, all you'll hear is crunching

and it won't bother your ears so much."

"Now that's enough."

Dad's voice is like sharp fish bones in my hot chocolate.

Grownups must not be able to think straight in the morning.

Because if I can't talk about Jerome anymore...

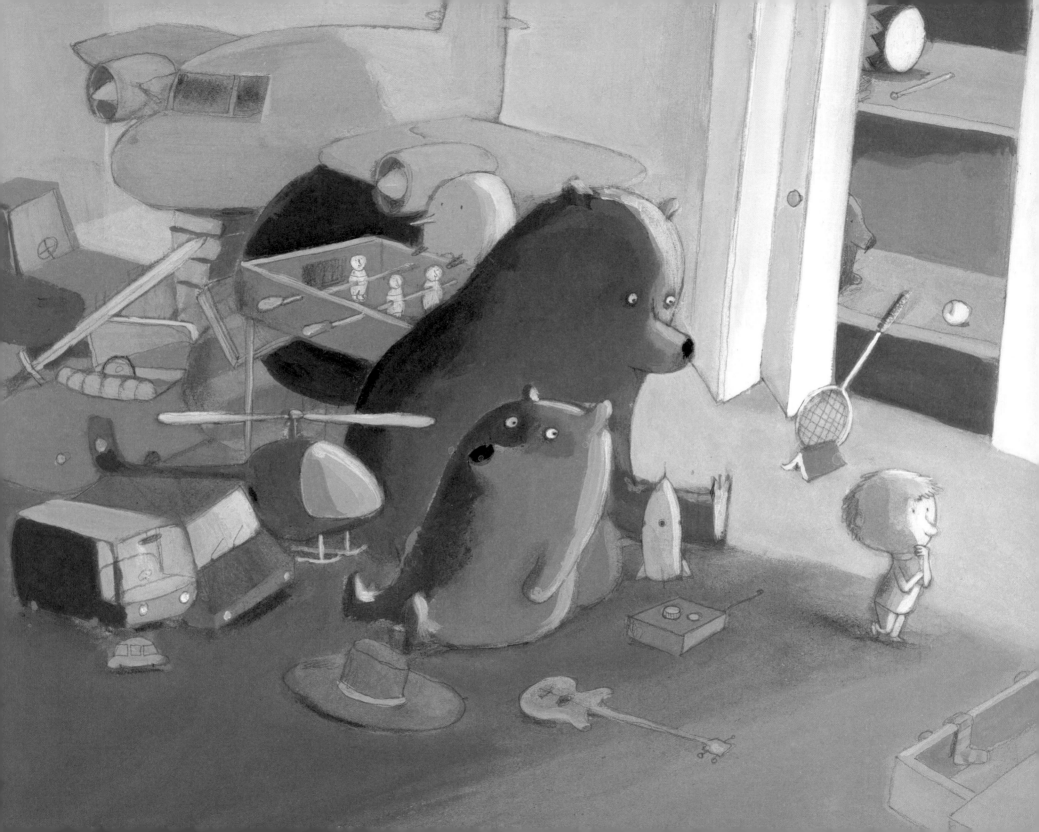

It's not like Jerome is a bad word.

I swallow my smile
and go to my room
to calm down.

I have to find a present for Jerome.
Something strong as a fortress
that will last forever.

I ransack my room.
I dump out my drawers.
I have to find the perfect thing.

I ransack my room because Jerome
says he'll go on vacation with me!
Maybe even to the highest peak of the Himalayas.
Anytime.

If I said we should build a race car,
he would jump right in.

And if he fell down and broke his arm
and cried in front of the whole world,
he still wouldn't hide his eyes in his shoelaces.

I circle around and around my bed.

Around and around my table.

Around and around my questions.

I forget my mom and dad.
I think only about Jerome,
who I know by heart.

And I say—yes.
Raphael loves Jerome.
I can say it.
It's easy.